Little Ballerinas

Grosset & Dunlap

To my beloved Tom—N.S.

Special thanks to Donna Estes, director of Donna's Dance Studio in Lynn, MA, assistants, parents, and especially all the little ballerinas.

Thanks also to Art Stone for providing ballerinas with tutus, leotards, and ballet slippers; "After the Stork" for children's clothes; Mark Hunt for backdrops and stage scenery; and Holy Family Church for recital stage.

Library of Congress Cataloging-in-Publication Data

Morris, Ann, 1930-
    Little ballerinas / by Ann Morris : photographs by Nancy Sheehan.
        p. cm
    Summary: Photographs and simple text follow some young ballet dancers from preparation for class through a recital.
    1. Ballet dancing—Juvenile literature. 2. Ballerinas—Juvenile literature. [1. Ballet dancing.]
    I. Sheehan, Nancy, ill. II. Title. III. Series.
        GV1787.5.M588 1997
        792.8'083'42—dc21   96-51475
                                                                                         CIP
ISBN 0-448-41607-7   F G H I J   AC

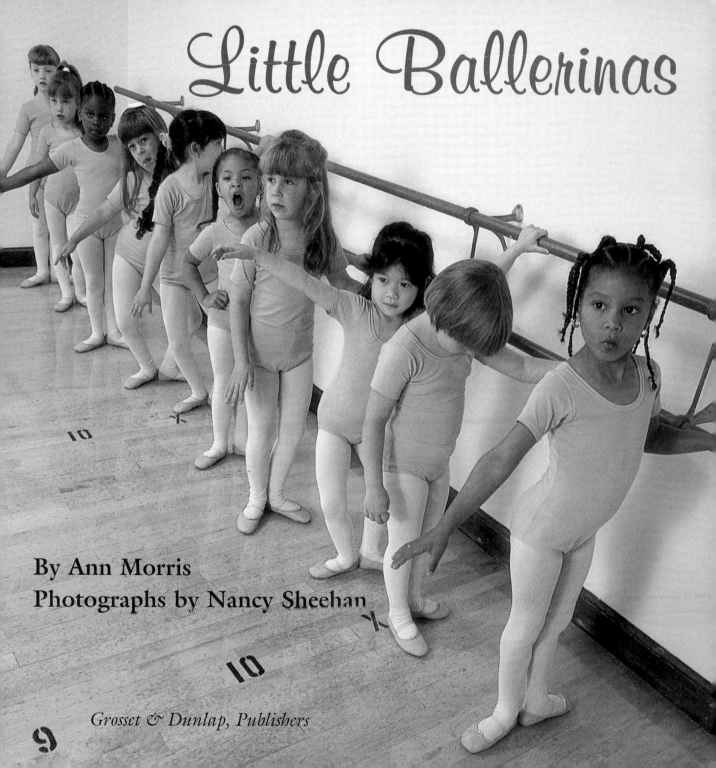

Little Ballerinas

By Ann Morris

Photographs by Nancy Sheehan

Grosset & Dunlap, Publishers

Look what Emily can do! She learned it at ballet school.
She is practicing in the kitchen to get ready for her class
today. "I can dance, too!" says her little sister.

Rachel goes to the same ballet school. She is in Emily's class.
"Let's brush your hair into a ponytail," says Rachel's father.
"It will stay out of your way while you're dancing."

Julie can't wait to
get to class. She even
dances while she
brushes her teeth.

Finally, off they all go to the studio. They carry their dance clothes and shoes in a special bag. They skip up the ramp. They skip through the door.

Inside they get into their leotards. Now they look like little ballerinas! First, they go to the *barre*, a long pole along the wall. At the *barre*, they do exercises to warm up and make their bodies strong.

The teacher helps them learn special dance steps and positions.

"Point your toe like this," she says. "Very good!"

"Now bend your knees. This is called a *plié*."

The teacher shows Marikka
how to turn her leg out.
   "You did that so well," she says.
And she gives Marikka a big hug.

Good friends are made at ballet school.

They dance together...

and have fun together.

They help each other, too.
"Can you show me how to stretch?" asks Julie.
"Like this," says Emily.

The little ballerinas are proud of what they can do.

They have worked very hard. Now they are ready
to put on a show.

On the day of the big performance, they get out their pretty pink tutus...

...and put them on.
How do I look?" says Allison.

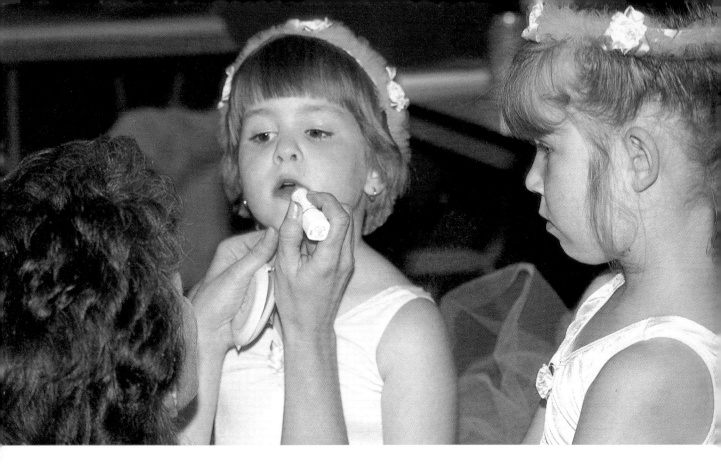

A little makeup will give their faces color under the bright stage lights. Some lipstick...

a touch of blush...

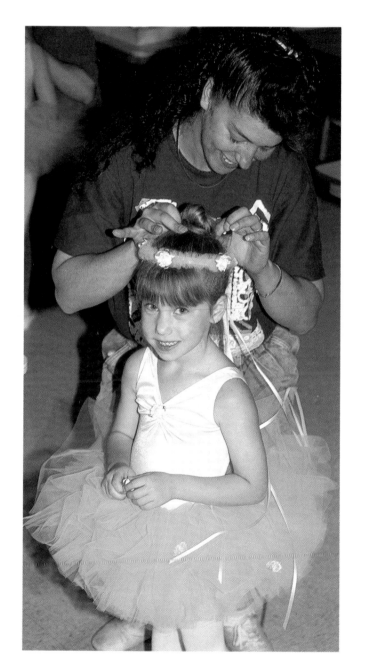

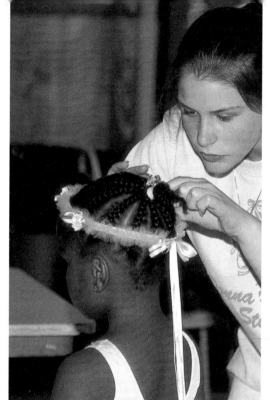

...and a beautiful crown with tiny pink flowers.

They feel very grown-up!

"Will I remember my steps?" thinks Nicole.

"Will they like my dance?" wonders Jessica.

The children are feeling happy and excited. Now they can show their parents and friends all the things they have learned!

The music begins. Each ballerina waits for her turn to go onstage.

They dance together.

They dance their very best.
They dance and dance!

When the show is over, they take a bow. Everyone claps.
"BRAVO!" they call out.
That means "Hooray! You were wonderful!"

The parents are proud of their little ballerinas. There are lots of pictures to be taken.

There are lots of hugs–
and lots of flowers, too!

Wouldn't you like
to be a ballerina?